MAHQGOA99

First published in the United States 1991
by Dial Books for Young Readers
A Division of Penguin Books USA Inc.
375 Hudson Street, New York, New York 10014

A Vanessa Hamilton Book
Printed in Portugal
First Edition
1 3 5 7 9 10 8 6 4 2
Library of Congress Cataloging in Publication Data
Mahy, Margaret.
The Queen's goat / story by Margaret Mahy;
pictures by Emma Chichester Clark.
p.   cm.
Summary: A young queen and her runaway goat make quite a
showing at the pet fair, where they win an unexpected prize.
ISBN 0-8037-0938-2
[1. Goats—Fiction. 2. Kings, queens, rulers, etc.—Fiction.
3. Pets—Fiction. 4. Contests—Fiction.]
I. Chichester Clark, Emma, ill. II. Title.
PZ7.M2773QU 1991 [E]—dc20 90-46717 CIP AC

MARGARET MAHY
The Queen's Goat

Illustrated by
EMMA CHICHESTER CLARK

Dial Books for Young Readers
New York

There was once a queen who had no pets. She was not allowed to have cats because cats spread cat hair on the cushions. She was not allowed to have dogs because dogs tracked mud all over the palace.

"No pets!" said the housekeeper firmly.

"No pets!" echoed the butler.

Outside near the castle orchard there was a white goat that belonged to the gardener. The goat's name was Carmen. Carmen was not a pet. She was a working goat. Her job was to keep the grass around the edge of the orchard short and neat. Every day the gardener moved Carmen's goathouse to another grassy spot.

The Queen enjoyed visiting Carmen and gave her bread crusts saved from breakfast (even though queens are supposed to eat their crusts to make their hair curl). She noticed that Carmen often stood on top of her goathouse looking longingly toward the distant mountains.

"When I am a grown-up queen," the Queen promised Carmen, "you and I will go to those mountains."

One day a special-looking letter was delivered to the Queen.
It said that a pet show would be held in the park and invited the
Queen to join the great parade with her pet. There would be
prizes for the wettest pet, the driest pet, the brightest pet, and
the funniest pet. There would also be prizes for the shyest
crocodile and the fiercest mouse.

"Oh, what a shame you can't go, Your Majesty," said the butler, reading over her shoulder (which was not very polite). "You don't have a pet. But never mind. At least there is no cat hair on the cushions!"

The Queen was nevertheless determined to go to the pet show. Putting on her best clothes, as well as her crown (held on straight with special elastic), out she went. She found the gardener having a quick snooze under an apple tree, while Carmen stood on her goathouse looking longingly toward the mountains.

"You and I are going to the pet show," announced the Queen, unhooking Carmen's chain.

The moment she was loose, Carmen took off like a hairy rocket and headed straight for the distant mountains.

Carmen was extremely strong, but a good queen knows how to hang on tightly, so off they went.

They whizzed through the royal petunias, then went
bumpity-bump-bump-bump across the lawn, under the
flowering cherry trees, and through the hedge into
Mrs. Zingler's backyard. Mrs. Zingler was hanging the
clothes on the line when something unexpected struck,
whirling her around thirty-two times.

"Heavens above!" she shrieked, staggering around in dizzy circles. "What was that? Where's my lace petticoat? Where are my husband's bright red long johns?"

But the Queen and Carmen were already speeding through Admiral Tompkins's garden. The Admiral had given himself a flagpole for his birthday. It stood in the middle of the garden. Admiral Tompkins was in the act of raising a whole string of naval flags when—*Whizzzz!*

Something covered in petunias and wearing a lace petticoat and bright red long johns knocked his feet right out from under him.

"Thunderation!" he cried. "What on earth was that? It has carried off all my favorite flags."

But the Queen and Carmen had whisked over his fence and onto the patio where Mr. and Mrs. Flip, the ballroom dancers, were practicing a complicated dance with tambourines.

Something sent them spinning into the air.
"Horrakapotchkin!" cried Mrs. Flip. "Whatever it was has taken our two tambourines!"

But not for a moment did the Queen and Carmen stop. They splashed through the stream on the other side of the patio, still speeding toward the distant mountains. Fortunately the park was in the same direction as the mountains. Though Carmen may not have realized it, she was heading straight for the pet show, dragging the Queen behind her.

Faster than bullets they shot under the ladder
Mr. Wallace was using to clean his windows.
His rag was an old satin nightgown that his wife
had put in the rag bag.

Mr. Wallace flew one way. His ladder flew another.

"Mercy!" cried Mr. Wallace, his bald head covered with soapy water. "What was that? And what has happened to my satin cleaning rag?"

There was no reply, since Carmen and the Queen had already dashed off toward the park.

But even an energetic goat like Carmen eventually had to slow down. Petunias were tangled around her ears, and a tambourine was impaled on each horn. She was wearing red long johns, a frilly lace petticoat, and draped gracefully around her neck, a satin nightgown, as well as several naval flags—all most unsuitable for a goat. Luckily the Queen (clinging desperately to

the chain) was surprisingly strong for such a small monarch.

"Carmen," cried the Queen, catching her breath. "Remember the pet show!"

Carmen gave one last, lingering look at the distant mountains. That look said, "I've done my best, but I'll never get there now!"

Then through the park gates she came at a steady trot, with the Queen running along behind her. By a remarkable coincidence they were just in time to join the great parade. Exhausted from dragging royalty through a bed of petunias and four gardens, Carmen behaved perfectly.

People exclaimed in pleasure at the sight of the well-dressed goat. Mrs. Zingler, Admiral Tompkins, Mr. and Mrs. Flip, not to mention Mr. Wallace—all of whom had run wildly after Carmen and the Queen—now stood in a row under the trees, wide-eyed with admiration and somewhat out of breath.

Carmen wasn't the wettest pet, nor was she the driest. She wasn't the brightest or the funniest. Anyone could see at a glance she wasn't a crocodile or a mouse. All the same, she did win a prize.

"A gold cup for the best-dressed pet in the parade!" announced the Mayor.

Everyone clapped loudly, especially Mrs. Zingler, Admiral Tompkins, Mr. and Mrs. Flip, and Mr. Wallace—thrilled to see their clothes and flags and tambourines displayed on such a distinguished goat.

After a triumph like that, Carmen became the official royal mascot. She did not leave hair on the cushions, though she did sometimes eat them. And once a year the Queen and Carmen went on vacation to the distant mountains, while the housekeeper and the butler stayed behind to polish the gold cup.